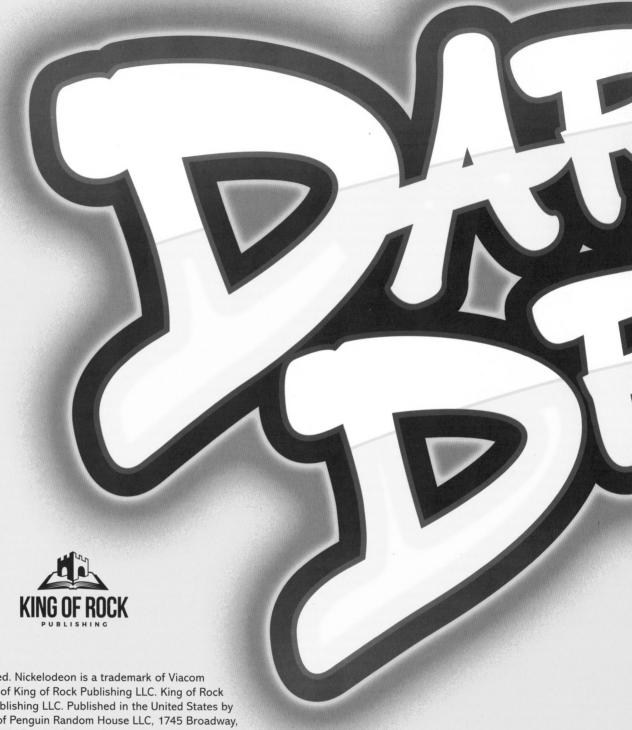

Dedicated to my wife, Zuri, and my son, D'Son—who have shown me the true joys of living.

Special thanks to Erik Blam, Cindy Baah, Pam Kaufman, and Makeda Mays Green for their hard work in making *Darryl's Dream* a reality.

—Darryl "DMC" McDaniels

Random House New York

rhcbooks.com

ISBN 978-0-593-48774-7 (trade) — ISBN 978-0-593-48830-0 (ebook)

MANUFACTURED IN CHINA

10 9 8 7 6 5 4 3

Random House Children's Books supports the First Amendment and celebrates the right to read.

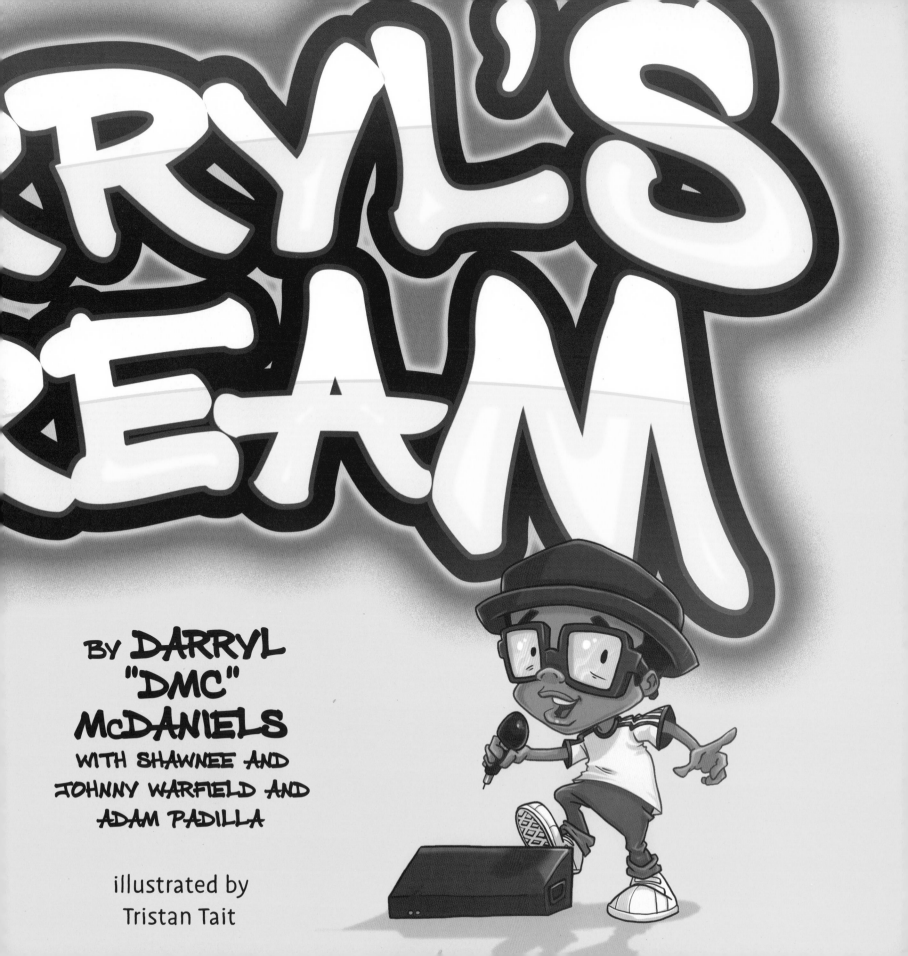

RYL'S
EAM

BY DARRYL "DMC" McDANIELS
WITH SHAWNEE AND JOHNNY WARFIELD AND ADAM PADILLA

illustrated by
Tristan Tait

DARRYL loved third grade. He especially loved music class and writing.

"Great job, Darryl!" said his teacher as she handed back his poem. There was a big A+ on it. "You should recite this at the talent show!"

"Really?" asked Darryl. He was proud of his poem, but he wondered—was it really that good?

After school, Darryl headed to the talent show sign-up sheet.
He wrote his name at the very bottom.

"What do you think you're doing?" said a boy named Charlie.
"What talent do *you* have?"

Darryl didn't know what to say, so he held up his poem.

"WOW! WHAT A NERD,"

said Charlie. "And you have
the dumb glasses to match."

A girl named Denise joined in. "Look, guys! Darryl's so weird with his stupid poems and his stupid A+. He's going to make a fool out of himself at the talent show!"

Everyone laughed. Darryl was so upset that he crossed his name off the sheet.

By the time Darryl got home, he felt totally defeated. "Mom," he said, "I wish I didn't wear big glasses and get good grades. The other kids don't like me."

"Not everyone will like you, Darryl," his mom said. "What's important is that you like yourself and you stay true to who you are."

Darryl didn't agree. He ran upstairs into his room.

"I wish I could be someone else," said Darryl as he fell asleep that night. Before long, he drifted off into a dream. . . .

DARRYL'S DREAM WAS AMAZING.

He flew all the way through space and up to the stars.

"Hello, Darryl," said a voice that echoed all around him.

"Here, you can be anyone or anything you want. Just wish it."

"I wish those mean kids liked me," said Darryl.

"As you wish," said the voice.

Suddenly, Darryl was big and strong. He was hanging out with the kids who'd made fun of him! But something was wrong. Darryl didn't feel like himself. He thought of another wish.

"I want to be something everyone likes," said Darryl.
"Like the coolest sports car in the world!"
"As you wish," said the voice.

Darryl turned into a supercharged hot rod. He looked amazing. People stood around him and admired his shiny new finish. Then he heard a noise from above.

"Look, a helicopter!" said someone in the crowd. It didn't take long before everyone forgot about Darryl.

"Wow," said Darryl. "Even the best hot rod isn't a helicopter. Guess I'd better wish for something else."
Darryl thought for a moment before he had an idea.
"I wish to be the best version of myself."
"As you wish," said the voice.

Suddenly, Darryl found himself inside a recording studio. There were instruments everywhere, and there was lots of fancy equipment. The walls were lined with gold records. Darryl looked at one of the awards and saw . . .

HIMSELF!

In the picture, he was grown up. He still had his glasses, and he looked cool in them.

Darryl was about to pick up a drumstick, when he heard a loud ringing.

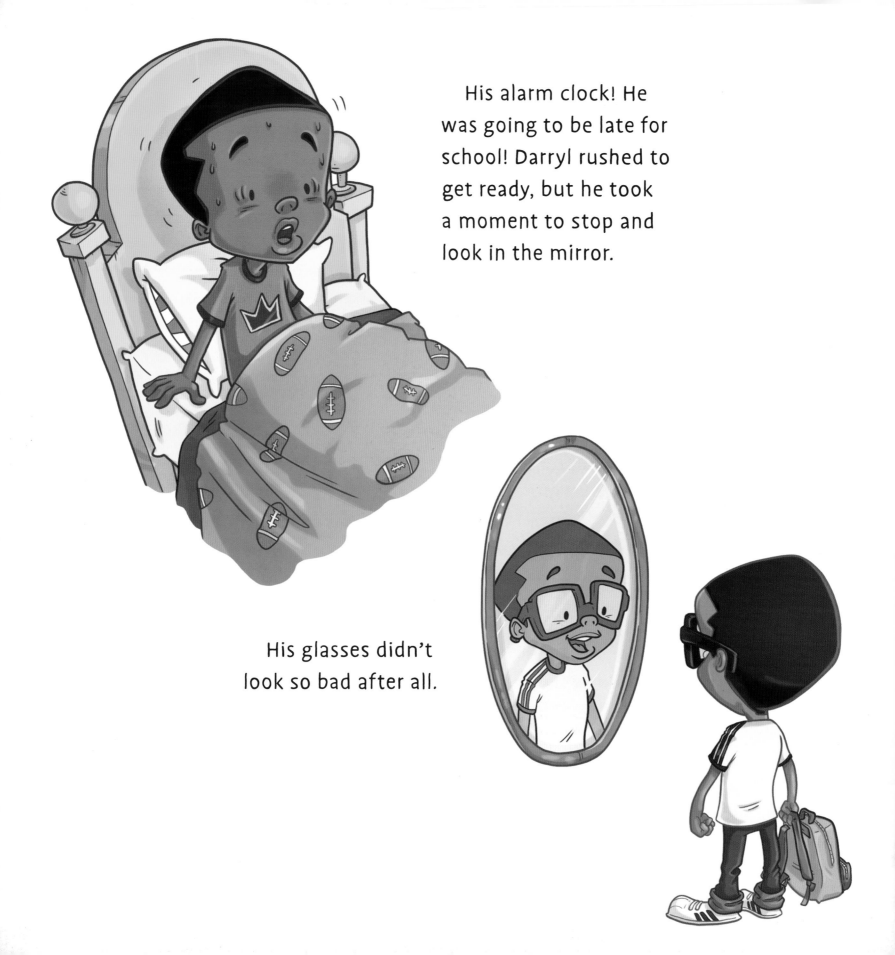

His alarm clock! He was going to be late for school! Darryl rushed to get ready, but he took a moment to stop and look in the mirror.

His glasses didn't look so bad after all.

"Ready for school?" asked his mom.

"MORE THAN EVER!"

said Darryl. He grabbed his poem and ran out the door.

Outside school, Darryl saw the kids who had picked on him making fun of another smart kid.

"STOP THAT!" said Darryl. "You guys think you're so cool, but you aren't."

At school, Darryl marched to the sign-up
sheet and put his name back on it. "I'm going
to do my poem at the talent show, and I don't
care what anyone thinks!"

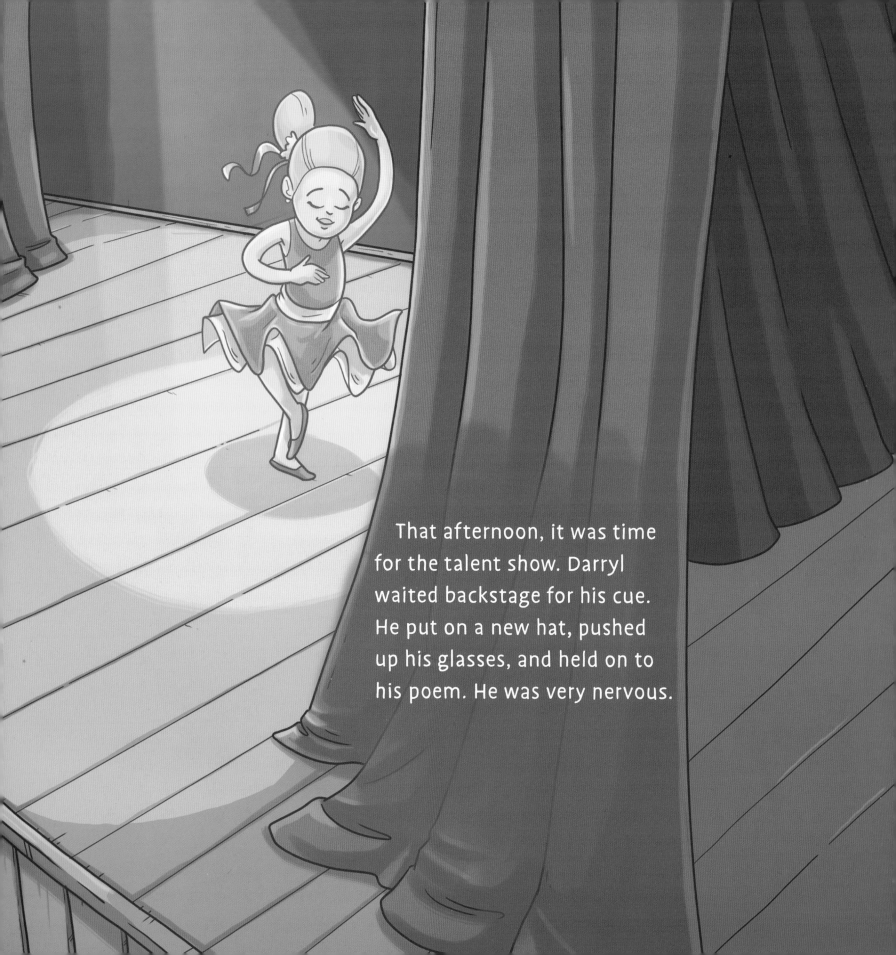

That afternoon, it was time for the talent show. Darryl waited backstage for his cue. He put on a new hat, pushed up his glasses, and held on to his poem. He was very nervous.

As he was waiting, the mean kids came backstage.

"You can't perform without your poem!" said Charlie. He grabbed the paper from Darryl and ripped it up.

"Yeah, and you look silly in that hat!" Denise chimed in. All the kids laughed. Just when Darryl thought it couldn't get worse, he was called to the stage.

Darryl froze in the spotlight. What was he going to do?

He thought of what his mom had told him. *I can do this. I just need to be myself!*

Darryl took a deep breath and grabbed the microphone. He rhymed about reading comic books and drawing superheroes. He rhymed about loving school and making friends. He even rhymed about how one day, he would go to college. The crowd was shocked!

"WHAT A WEIRDO!" someone yelled.

But Darryl kept going. He rhymed about bullies and school. He rhymed about what his mom had taught him. He even rhymed about his glasses. As the words flowed out of him, the crowd rose to their feet, cheering.

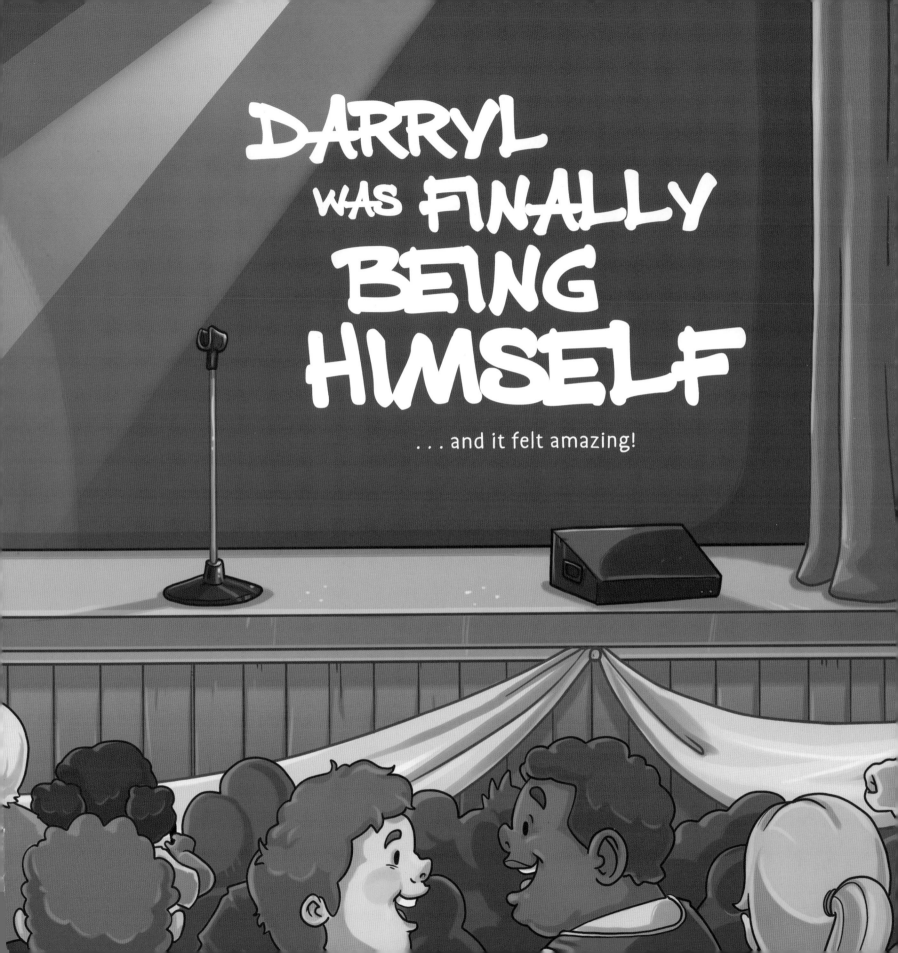

After the show, Darryl ran into Charlie and Denise.

"Wow, Darryl!" said Denise. "I didn't know poems could sound like that. That was really cool."

"Me neither," added Charlie. "Can you teach me how to write poems just like you?"

Darryl smiled. "I'll help you," he said, "but you shouldn't write poems like me. You should write poems like Charlie."

DARRYL McDANIELS

followed his dream and went on to become hip-hop pioneer DMC. He traveled the world spreading his personal style and message of love and confidence to millions. His glasses even became a symbol of hip-hop fashion! Darryl still loves music and continues to teach children to be themselves and follow their dreams.